SIMON & SCHUSTER BOOKS FOR YOUNG READERS • An imprint of Simon & Schuster Children's Publishing Division • 1230 Avenue of the Americas, New York, New York 10020 • Text copyright © 2012 by Michelle Meadows • Illustrations copyright © 2012 by Matthew Cordell • All rights reserved, including the right of reproduction in whole or in part in any form. • SIMON & SCHUSTER BOOKS FOR YOUNG READERS is a trademark of Simon & Schuster, Inc. • For information about special discounts for bulk purchases, please contact Simon & Schuster Special Sales at 1-866-506-1949 or business@simonandschuster.com. • The Simon & Schuster Speakers Bureau can bring authors to your live event. For more information or to book an event, contact the Simon & Schuster Speakers Bureau at 1-866-248-3049 or visit our website at www.simonspeakers .com. • Book design by Chloë Foglia • The text for this book is set in Bernhard Modern Std. • The illustrations for this book are rendered in pen and ink with watercolor. • Manufactured in China • 1211 SCP

2 4 6 8 10 9 7 5 3 1

Library of Congress Cataloging-in-Publication Data
Meadows, Michelle. • Itsy-bitsy baby mouse / Michelle Meadows ; illustrated by Matthew Cordell.
— 1st ed. • p. cm.
Summary: A baby mouse gets lost and experiences frightening adventures before finding his way back home to his parents. • ISBN 978-1-4169-3786-9 (hardcover)
[1. Stories in rhyme. 2. Lost children—Fiction. 3. Mice—Fiction.] I. Cordell, Matthew, 1975– ill.
II. Title. • PZ8.3.M4625It 2012 • [E]—dc22 • 2010023014

For Rosemary
Stimola, who
always points
me in the right
direction when
I get lost
—M. M.

FOR
Itsy-Bitsy
Baby Romy
—M. C.

MICHELLE MEADOWS

illustrated by

MATTHEW CORDELL

Simon & Schuster Books for Young Readers

NEW YORK   LONDON   TORONTO   SYDNEY

Itsy-bitsy
baby mouse.

Whirling, twirling
round the house.

Chase a busy,
buzzy fly.

Creep and leap and
reach up high.

Crispy crumbs of
apple pie!

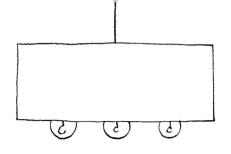

Wait a minute—

"Mama, Papa!

Are you there?"

Looking for them everywhere.

Weeping, creeping 'cross the rug.
Teensy-weensy ladybug.

Crawl up on a fuzzy mound.
Cozy pillow, soft and round.

Yikes! I'm moving!
What is *that*?

This pillow is a sleeping *cat*!

Tippy, tippy, tiptoe.
Slowly, slowly, uh-oh!

Run and roll and
rush to hide.

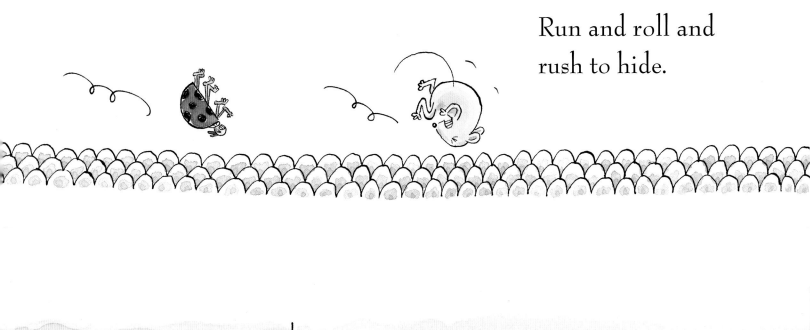

Clip a corner,

slip and slide.

Bump into a friendly mouse!
"Help me, please. I lost my house."

"Houses don't just disappear.
What's it look like? What's it near?"

"The door is red and near a tree.
It's underneath a giant key."

Climb up on a
wooden ledge.

Cross and hop down
off the edge.

Up ahead
I see the tree!
And look above,
a great big key!

Faster, faster, almost there.
Then someone lifts me in the air.

The pillow cat has
got my tail!
Close my eyes and
start to wail.

Kicking, screaming—

"No, no, no!

Have mercy, cat.

Please let me go!"

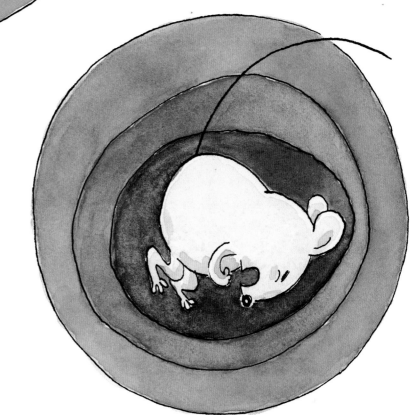

"Baby mouse, what's all the fuss?
Open up. It's only us.

You gave us such an awful scare.
We've been looking everywhere."

"Mama, Papa!"
Kiss and hug.
Baby mouse and
ladybug.